A Note to Parents and Teachers

Eyewitness Readers is a compelling new reading programme for children. *Eyewitness* has become the most trusted name in illustrated books, and this new series combines the highly visual *Eyewitness* approach with engaging, easy-to-read stories. Each *Eyewitness Reader* is guaranteed to capture a child's interest while developing his or her reading skills, general knowledge and love of reading.

The books are written by leading children's authors and are designed in conjunction with literacy experts, including Cliff Moon M.Ed., Honorary Fellow of the University of Reading. Cliff Moon spent many years as a teacher and teacher educator specializing in reading. He has written more than 140 books for children and teachers, and he reviews regularly for teachers' journals.

The four levels of *Eyewitness Readers* are aimed at different reading abilities, enabling you to choose the books that are exactly right for each child.

Level 1 – Beginning to read
Level 2 – Beginning to read alone
Level 3 – Reading alone
Level 4 – Proficient readers

The "normal" age at which a child begins to read can be anywhere from three to eight years old, so these levels are only guidelines. No matter which level you select, you can be sure that you're helping children learn to read, then read to learn!

A Dorling Kindersley Book
www.dk.com

Created by Leapfrog Press Ltd

Project Editor Naia Bray-Moffatt
Art Editor Jane Horne

For Dorling Kindersley
Senior Editor Linda Esposito
Senior Art Editor Diane Thistlethwaite
US Editor Regina Kahney
Production Josie Alabaster
Picture Researcher Liz Moore

Natural History Consultant
Theresa Greenaway
Reading Consultant
Cliff Moon M.Ed.

Published in Great Britain by
Dorling Kindersley Limited
9 Henrietta Street
London WC2E 8PS

4 6 8 10 9 7 5 3

Eyewitness Readers™ is a trademark of
Dorling Kindersley Limited, London.

A CIP catalogue record for this book is
available from the British Library.

ISBN 0 7513 5898 3

Colour reproduction by Colourscan, Singapore
Printed and bound in Belgium by Proost

The publisher would like to thank the following
for their kind permission to reproduce their photographs:
Key: t=top, a=above, b=below, l=left, r=right, c=centre

Bruce Coleman: Gordon Langsbury front cover c; **Dorling Kindersley Picture Library:** 1bl, 8–9tl, 20bl, 24tra, 24trb **/Andy Crawford:** 2br, 25 **/Frank Greenaway:** 1tl, 4cl, 9b, 18tr, 18-19b, 28tl, 29br **/Dave King:** 1cla, 1br, 2tr, cr, 10–11, 13tr, b, 18tl, 21br, 24c, 28cr**/Dave King/Natural History Museum:** 14bl, 14–15b, 16-17b, 16tr **/Susanna Price:** 15tr **/Matthew Ward:** 1cra, 22tr, trb; **NHPA:** 22–23b, 26br; **NHPA/Bill Coster:** 27; **Planet Earth Pictures: Mark Mattock** front cover tr, cl; **Telegraph Colour Library:** 3br, 4–5b, 6tr, 6-7b, 9tr, 12tr, 15tl, 17tr, 19tr, 21bl, 26, 31tr; **Tony Stone Images:** front cover background, 1tr, 5tr, 20–21t, 20tl; **Tony Stone/Frank Orel:** 30–31b; **Tony Stone Images/John Warden:** 1crb, 24br, bl

EYEWITNESS  READERS

A Day at Seagull Beach

Written by Karen Wallace

DK

DORLING KINDERSLEY
London • New York • Sydney • Moscow

On a cliff above the seashore,
two sharp-eyed seagulls
build a nest.
They gather sticks
and bits of seaweed.

They watch the children
on the sand.

One seagull soars above the ocean.
The waves crash
on the seashore.
Whoosh! Boom!

The seagull skims the salty water.
What is the seagull looking for?

Seaweed flutters underwater.
Some looks like leaves.
Some looks like ribbons.

The sharp-eyed seagull
dips and searches.
What is the seagull looking for?

Down on the seabed,
a flat fish swims.

WIGGLE! WIGGLE!
He hides among
the pebbles.

The seagull walks along the shoreline. TAP! TAP! He pecks a crab's hard shell.

SNAP! SNIP!
The crab waves
his sharp pincers.

What is the seagull looking for?

He hops behind
a slimy boulder.
He sees a rock pool
shining in the sun.

Inside the pool
a starfish creeps.

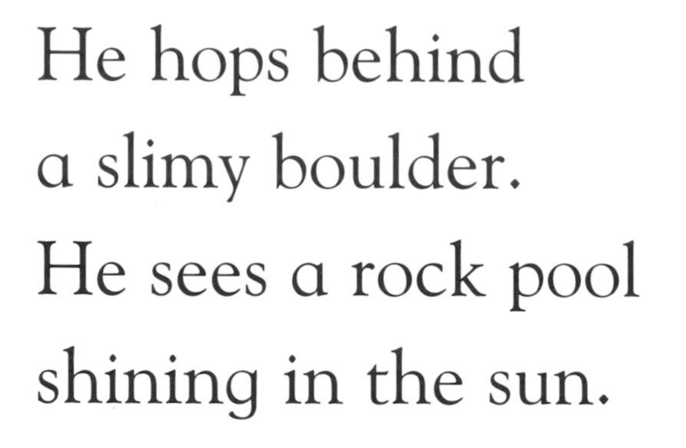

starfish

Nearby,
children laugh and play.

The sharp-eyed seagull
stands and watches.
A limpet clings to a salty stone.

What is the seagull looking for?

A crab hides
in the seaweed.
The seagull waits...

A pop-eyed prawn darts
through the water.

The seagull strikes!

His beak pushes
through the water.
Too late!
The pop-eyed
prawn escapes!

The tide goes out,
the waves fall back.
A sandcastle sits
on the shore.

The seagull hunts among the seaweed. What is the seagull looking for?

He pokes and pecks
the shiny seashells.
They crunch and
tumble in the waves.
Some are straight. Some are curly.
The seagull flips them
with his feet.

seashells

What is the seagull looking for?

He finds bits of glass
and polished stones.

He finds a hermit crab
and a jellyfish.

jellyfish

He sees a footprint in the sand.

What is the seagull looking for?

A fish tail flicks along a wave top.
Other seagulls swoop and cry.
SKREEK! SKREEK!

The seagull shrieks and snatches.
SNAP!
His beak is full of fish!

He's found
what he's been looking for!

On the cliff above the sea
the sharp-eyed seagull
lands by his mate.

She climbs off the nest.
He climbs on.
Two eggs are
lying underneath!

A seagull soars above the water.
She knows her eggs are
safe and warm.
She sees the children on the sand.

She skims along
the salty water.

What is the seagull looking for?

Picture Word List

seaweed
page 4

waves
page 20

pincer
page 13

seashells
page 22

starfish
page 14

jellyfish
page 24

limpet
page 16

eggs
page 28